Sometimes strange, unimaginable things happen that no-body can explain. They happen to ordinary people. Have you ever seen a UFO? Or had a dream at night that seemed so real—and it came true?

The stories in this book actually happened. You will read about:

- A businessman who saw nine saucer-like objects speeding through the sky

- Passengers on a ship who watched as another ship was dragged underwater by a sea monster

- A ten-foot-long dragonlike creature that attacked and ate a water buffalo in several large gulps

- A man who dreamed of an airplane crash that came true several days later

. . . and many more tales of the supernatural and unex-plained.

REMEMBER: The stories inside this book are true!

Strange Unsolved Mysteries from Tor Books

Mysteries of Ships and Planes
Monsters, Strange Dreams, and UFOs

STRANGE UNSOLVED MYSTERIES

MONSTERS, STRANGE DREAMS and UFOs

PHYLLIS RAYBIN EMERT

TOR

A TOM DOHERTY ASSOCIATES BOOK
NEW YORK

The author would like to thank
Helene Chirinian
and
Shara Gilman
for their help and support

Contents

II. Monsters

III. ESP and Other Mysteries

❦ I ❦
UFOs

Definition

Unidentified Flying Objects: any airborne object which by performance, aerodynamic characteristics, or unusual feature does not conform to any presently known aircraft or missile type, or which cannot be positively identified as a familiar object.

United States Air Force Regulation 200-2

Kenneth Arnold

Throughout history, people have seen strange objects in the sky. Many people were afraid, and others paid no attention. Kenneth Arnold changed all that. What he saw on the afternoon of June 24, 1947, marked the beginning of the "flying saucer" age in the United States.

Later, the term "UFO" was used to describe these mysterious things. The letters stood for "unidentified flying object."

In 1947, Kenneth Arnold was thirty-two years old and living in Boise, Idaho. He owned a fire-control equipment company and was also a pilot who flew his own single-engine plane.

On this day in June, a C-46 marine transport plane had crashed and was missing in the Cascade mountain range in the state of Washington. A $5,000 reward had been offered to locate it.

"What a beautiful afternoon for flying," he thought to himself. He had to fly to Yakima, Washington, on business, so he decided to search for the missing airplane along the way.

Arnold took off from the Chehalis, Washington, airport at 2 P.M. It was so clear he could see for miles in every direction. He was an experienced pilot and had flown over this area many times before.

After about an hour, Arnold was near Mount Rainier, the highest mountain peak in the Cascade Range.

"What was that!" he thought suddenly as a bright flash seemed to light up his plane. Arnold looked around. "There's a DC-4 back there to the left but it's too far away," he thought.

The flash came again. But this time Arnold noticed where it came from. Looking north he saw nine bright objects flying in two rows. He rubbed his eyes in amazement, but when he opened them, they were still there darting between the mountaintops.

Arnold was more than twenty miles away but saw the objects clearly. They were "flat like a pie pan and so shiny they reflected the sun like a mirror," he later told reporters. Their motion was "like speedboats on rough water. They flew like a saucer would if you skipped it across the water."

Arnold thought, "They're flying so fast." He knew that the distance between Mount Rainier and Mount Adams was forty-seven miles. It took the strange objects one minute and forty-two seconds to travel that distance.

"That's impossible," he said to himself. "They would have to be traveling more than sixteen hundred miles per hour! No airplane can travel that fast! Could they be some new kind of missile or weapon?"

When he landed at Yakima, he told his story to airport officials. By the time he flew on to Pendleton, Oregon, newsmen were already waiting to write about the incident in their papers.

Arnold was a respectable businessman and pilot. He was no quack. The reporters wrote about the sighting in a serious way, but they used his "saucer" description in the article. The story was picked up by newspapers all over the world. Soon, headlines began referring to the objects as "flying saucers."

Public interest grew and the United States Air Force became involved in the investigation. It wanted to be sure that the objects weren't some sort of secret weapon which could be used against the United States.

But people began to doubt Arnold's story. They made fun of the term "flying saucers." Some said he made up the whole incident.

Arnold wrote an article in the first issue of a new magazine called *Fate*. It was called "I Did See the Flying Discs." He later said angrily, "I'm absolutely certain of what I saw! But, believe me, if I ever see a phenomenon of that sort in the sky again, I won't say a word about it!"

Arnold's treatment set the tone for those who later reported seeing unidentified flying objects. They were made fun of and joked about.

Many did take the sightings seriously. The Air Force studied each reported sighting, and these investigations were known as Project Sign (then Project Grudge in 1949 and finally Project Blue Book in 1952).

What were the nine shiny objects in the sky that Kenneth Arnold saw that day? The Air Force wasn't sure. Was Kenneth Arnold imagining it all or did he see strange-shaped objects in the sky?

On July 4, ten days after the sighting by Arnold, the crew of a United Airlines plane saw five, then four more disclike objects in the sky over Boise, Idaho. Captain E. J. Smith and copilot Ralph Stevens said the nine objects then flew away at a high rate of speed.

Were they spacecraft from another planet or just the sun reflecting off the cockpit window? To this day, no one knows for certain.

Clarence Chiles
and John Whitted

It was a routine flight for the Eastern Airlines DC-3. The airplane was headed to Atlanta, Georgia, carrying twenty-one passengers on July 24, 1948.

The pilot and copilot were experienced airmen. Clarence Chiles was a veteran of World War II and had flown more than eight thousand hours. His copilot, John Whitted, was also an experienced flier.

The DC-3 flew at five thousand feet through a clear, moonlit sky. It was 2:45 in the morning when they passed near Montgomery, Alabama.

"Look," said Captain Chiles suddenly. "Here comes some new kind of jet." They saw what seemed to be a large aircraft heading right toward them.

"I'll try to turn out or we'll crash into it!" he shouted to Whitted. The other craft flew at a high rate of speed and passed the DC-3 on the right, only seven hundred feet away. Then it pulled up suddenly and seemed to disappear in a few clouds.

"Where did it go?" asked Whitted as he looked around. "It must have been traveling more than five hundred miles per hour!"

Chiles was amazed. "Did you see it had no wings?"

Whitted nodded. "I saw flames shooting out of the back."

Both men had only seen the mysterious craft for ten to fifteen seconds but they agreed on the way it looked. It was about one hundred feet long and twenty-five to thirty feet wide. It had no fins or wings and was the shape of a cigar. The object had two rows of windows and a dark blue glow.

Both men noticed orange-red flames trailing out the back as it pulled up. But there was no noise or air movement from the craft as it passed them.

With most of the passengers aboard the DC-3 asleep, only one passenger, C. L. McKelvie claimed to have seen a bright streak of light passing his window at a high rate of speed.

The two airmen reported their story to airline officials. The incident made headlines in newspapers around the country. One front-page headline in the *Atlanta Constitution* read, "Atlanta Pilots Report Wingless Sky Monster."

Chiles was convinced that the strange aircraft had some kind of intelligent control. He believed that it purposely pulled up sharply to avoid the risk of crashing into the DC-3.

Air Force investigators questioned Chiles, Whitted, and passenger McKelvie. They checked to see if any other plane had been in the air that night in their location. But none had.

The conclusion first reached by the Air Force was mixed. Some officials had no explanation. Others stated that it was a meteor. They thought that the rows of windows that Chiles and Whitted saw in the craft were actually the bright glow from the meteor, which then burned up before it reached the Earth's surface.

After a time, the Air Force adopted the meteor story and closed the case. Years later, UFO investigator Philip Klass supported this conclusion. In his book *UFOs Explained* (1974), he wrote that there was a meteor shower that week in 1948.

Klass feels that intelligent people who see something strange and unexpected may have trouble describing what they see. He referred to a case that happened twenty years after the Chiles-Whitted sighting. In 1968, witnesses described a strange cigar-shaped craft with windows very much like the one Chiles and Whitted had seen. It turned out to be flaming pieces of a Russian rocket booster which fell to Earth.

Chiles and Whitted stuck to their belief that they had seen an unidentified flying object and not a meteor. Both pilots felt they were experienced and calm enough to be able to tell the difference between the two. They believed that a meteor couldn't pull up sharply to avoid a collision.

Was there some type of intelligence controlling the mysterious craft in 1948? If so, where did it come from? Or did the two pilots actually see a meteor flash by, but mistake it for something else? You be the judge.

Washington, D.C.

There was an uncomfortable heat wave in Washington, D.C., on Saturday, July 19, 1952. Everyone tried to keep cool, including the air traffic controllers at Washington National Airport.

Aircraft traffic was light that Saturday night at 11:40, and there wasn't a cloud in the sky.

Suddenly, Ed Nugent saw seven strange blips on his radar screen. "What do you make of this, Harry?" he asked his supervisor.

Harry Barnes was the senior controller for the Civil Aeronautics Agency (CAA). Barnes came over to take a look. He saw seven light violet spots grouped together in one corner of the screen.

"This is strange, Ed. They're in the air about fifteen miles south of the city," said Barnes.

"I figure they're moving between a hundred and a hundred thirty miles per hour,'' replied Nugent, ''and then they zip away at higher speeds.''

''They're not traveling like ordinary airplanes,'' stated Barnes, ''and they're not in any formation. Get Ritchey and Copeland over to take a look.''

Jim Ritchey and Jim Copeland, two experienced controllers, also saw the blips and agreed that these were not regular airplanes.

The radar screen at the airport control tower showed the same seven blips. After a quick check, Barnes was sure the equipment was operating correctly. Then he called the Air Force to tell them about the unidentified flying objects.

A number of airplane pilots reported seeing strange lights moving all over the sky. The lights slowed, stopped, and then sped away in different directions. These sightings all showed up on the airport radar screens as well as on those at nearby Andrews Air Force Base. Ground crews at the airport also reported seeing a ''bright, orange light.''

Finally, at 3 A.M., Air Force jets arrived to investigate. As the jets came close, the objects disappeared from the radar screens and the pilots saw nothing. When the jets left the area to return to their base, the blips popped up again on the screens. Some were even over the White House and Capitol building.

Airplane and ground crews continued seeing the mysterious lights all through the morning hours of July 20. Radar screens at the airport and Andrews Air Force Base kept tracking them. At one point, radio operators at Andrews ran outside to see a round red-orange object above them in the sky.

By daybreak, the blips disappeared. Reporters found out what had happened and there were articles in newspapers all over the country. Headlines read, ''The Day the Saucers Visited Washington D.C.'' and ''Jets Lose Race With Glowing Globs.''

But it wasn't over yet. Exactly one week later, on Saturday, July 26, at 9 P.M., the blips returned. And again radar screens at Andrews and the airport tracked them.

Barnes called the Air Force, and at 11:25 P.M., F-94 jets flew in for a look. As the jets arrived, the blips disappeared. At about the same time, reports from nearby Virginia came in describing strange lights over their area.

More jets were ordered in. This time, one of the pilots spotted a light and then it vanished. The pilot said it was ''like somebody turning off a light bulb'' when he flew closer. When the jet returned to base, the blips showed up again on the radar screens.

During the next few hours, airplane crews reported seeing lights, as did ground crew members and many other people.

Again, newspaper headlines told of the flying saucer invasion over Washington. Even the President of the United States, Harry Truman, wanted to know what was happening. The Air Force was flooded with calls about the UFOs. People were getting scared!

On July 29, the Air Force Director of Intelligence called a press conference. He assured everyone that the sightings were not a threat to the United States and that the objects were not any type of secret weapon.

The director explained that the blips on radar were the result of a ''temperature inversion.'' There was a layer of cool air between layers of hot dry air and warm humid air. This could cause light reflections from the ground which would show up on the radar screens.

Many people disagreed with the Air Force's explanation. The radar operators noticed weather blips on the screen caused by a temperature inversion. But they said that they easily saw the difference on their screens between the UFO blips and these weather blips.

What about the strange sightings by the airliner and ground crews and even the pilot of the jet? The Air Force explained that a temperature inversion can also cause mirages—when people see something that isn't there.

But there are many unanswered questions. Can temperature inversions appear and then disappear, as the objects did, when Air Force jets fly too close?

Did the strange lights act as if they were controlled by some type of intelligence?

Were the mysterious moving lights and objects just a trick of the imagination, even though so many people claimed to have seen them?

Many people accepted the Air Force's explanation for the incident in Washington. Others felt that the Air Force covered up because they had no other way to explain what had happened.

If it wasn't the weather that caused the radar and visual sightings, then what (or who) was it?

Officers Carson
and Scott

"Look out there!" shouted California Highway Patrol Officer C. A. Carson excitedly to his partner. He pointed just ahead of their car. "It's a plane about to crash!"

"Pull over quickly," answered Officer S. Scott. "Maybe we can do something to help."

They were driving on a back road south of Red Bluff, in Northern California, at about 11 P.M. It was August 13, 1960.

They stopped their patrol car and jumped out ready to help with the disaster. But instead of a plane, the two men saw a long metallic object suddenly stop in midair. Then it climbed back up to several hundred feet and stopped again.

"It's moving toward us," Carson whispered, "but I don't hear any engines."

They both had their pistols out. "I'm ready to fire if I need to," said Scott quietly.

Suddenly, the mysterious object stopped about one hundred to two hundred feet away. Scott tried to radio back to headquarters, but there was strong interference and he couldn't get through.

The officers looked closely at the strange craft. It had large bright lights at each end. Carson estimated that one was six feet across. There were also smaller lights all over the body of the object.

After a few minutes, it started moving away. The men tried their radio again and this time it worked. They asked for backup patrol cars and requested a check with the nearby Red Bluff Air Force Radar Station.

After the call, the officers began to follow the unidentified aircraft. Other witnesses saw the UFO in different locations throughout the county. Air Force Radar said they were tracking an unknown object. Scott and Carson followed the craft for two more hours before it disappeared.

The next day the radar station said no sighting had been made. When Carson and Scott asked to talk to the operator who had been on duty, their request was turned down.

Project Blue Book, the Air Force unit that investigates UFOs, later stated that the two officers had really seen "a refraction (bending of light rays) of the planet Mars and two bright stars." They had not seen an unidentified flying object.

But astronomers found that neither Mars nor the two stars were visible in Northern California that night. Then Project Blue Book changed its statement, saying that the officers saw Mars and Capella, another bright star. Yet Capella was nowhere near the strange object that Carson and Scott followed.

Could these two experienced police officers mistake a planet and star in the sky for an object one hundred to two hundred feet away? Could Mars or Capella dive toward the ground, stop, and then climb back up into the sky?

Carson was quoted as saying, "No one will ever convince us that we were witnessing a refraction of light."

Was there a cover-up by the Air Force about this close and detailed sighting? Or did Carson and Scott see the bright lights in the sky and, in their excitement, mistake them for a UFO?

The Air Force officially lists this sighting as "identified."

Betty and Barney Hill

"What is that strange light in the sky?" Betty Hill asked her husband, Barney. "It's getting bigger and brighter."

The Hills were headed home to Portsmouth, New Hampshire, after a vacation in Niagara Falls, New York. They were driving along Highway 3 late on the night of September 19, 1961.

"It's following us, Barney!" yelled Betty. She had been looking at the bright object through binoculars. "You've got to stop the car and take a look!"

"All right," answered Barney, who thought it was just an airplane or helicopter. He wanted to calm his wife down.

Barney stopped the car but left the engine running. They were in the White Mountains on a deserted stretch of road. He took the binoculars from his wife, opened the car door, and stepped out on the highway.

As he watched the object, now only about one hundred feet away, it began to come down slowly. It was glowing and there was no noise at all. There seemed to be a row of windows, and through them, Barney could see some type of beings watching him.

They were dressed all in black. Some were busy controlling the craft. He noticed that two red lights on two side fins of the object had suddenly appeared.

"I don't believe it!" said Barney, beginning to panic. "This is ridiculous!"

He became frightened. "These are not humans," Barney thought to himself.

"We're going to be caught like a bug in a net," he told Betty. "Let's get out of here!" he yelled as he jumped into the car and sped off down the highway.

Then the Hills heard strange beeping sounds coming from the back end of the car. The next thing they knew, they were passing a sign that read "Concord—17 miles." When they arrived home in Portsmouth, they realized the trip had taken two hours longer than usual.

The next day, Betty told her sister they had seen a UFO. She even wrote to the National Investigations Committee on Aerial Phenomena (NICAP). In her letter she described what she and Barney had seen.

Ten days later, Betty began having terrible nightmares. She dreamed that she and Barney had been taken aboard an alien spacecraft and examined. Barney was also upset. He was tense, had headaches, and couldn't sleep.

After being treated by a doctor for over a year with no success, they were referred to a psychiatrist named Benjamin Simon. Dr. Simon used hypnosis in treating his patients.

After six months of treatment, Betty and Barney finally

remembered what happened to them during those two extra hours.

In separate sessions under hypnosis, Barney and Betty related their experiences. They said that their car had stopped and black-clothed alien beings had surrounded them.

Their faces were ugly. They had large heads and two slits for a nose. Their long, thin eyes extended around the sides of their faces. But they used telepathy (mind communication) to tell the Hills not to be afraid.

Barney and Betty were taken up a ramp and into the spacecraft. Each was examined in a separate room, as a doctor might give a patient a checkup.

The aliens took samples of their hair, skin scrapings, and parts of their fingernails. They used needles and strange-looking machines on different parts of their bodies. It was very uncomfortable.

Both Betty and Barney told the same basic story. They were recorded on tape in separate sessions by Dr. Simon. But Betty was able to give a more detailed description of their experience. Barney couldn't remember many details.

Betty asked the "leader" of the aliens where he came from. The leader showed her a star map, which Betty later drew for Dr. Simon.

The Hills were then taken back to their car and heard the strange beeps. The next thing they remembered was seeing the Concord mileage sign.

As the Hills' story became known to the public, it received much attention. The incident was written up in *Look* magazine. A book by John Fuller called *The Interrupted Journey* was published in 1966. A movie about the Hills' experience called *The UFO Incident* was first shown on television on October 20, 1975.

The Hills were intelligent, sincere, and responsible people. Betty was a social worker for the state of New Hampshire. She appeared on radio and TV shows and spoke at colleges and conferences about her experience. Barney was a member of the State Advisory Board of the U.S. Civil Rights Commission. He died in 1969 of a brain hemorrhage at the age of forty-six.

There have been many questions about the Hill case over the years.

Robert Sheaffer, author of *The UFO Verdict*, believes that Betty and Barney saw Jupiter and Saturn that night in 1961 and not a spacecraft. The two planets were very big and bright in the sky at the time.

The exact time of night that the Hills sighted the object is still unclear. Different accounts give different times. Another problem is that the Hills say the sky was clear when it was actually very cloudy.

Why did Betty give more details about what happened than Barney did? Robert Sheaffer believes that the story under hypnosis was just a retelling of Betty's nightmares. Barney had heard his wife's dreams many times. She often told them to friends and relatives. So he was just repeating Betty's story.

Can a person lie under hypnosis, or must he or she tell the truth? Experts in the field feel that what comes out under hypnosis is what the person *believes* really happened. But it's not always the truth. Even Dr. Simon, the Hills' psychiatrist, thinks their story was a fantasy that Betty and Barney shared.

But Pease Air Force Base in Portsmouth, New Hampshire, observed an ''unidentified target'' near the runway approach that night in 1961 at 2:14 A.M. Was that the alien spacecraft? Sheaffer says even birds can show up on radar as unknown objects.

If the Hills' experience was a shared fantasy, how could Betty have drawn the star map? She wasn't familiar with astronomy. Some experts say her map matches up with other stars that may have planets similar to Earth. Yet there are others who say the map matches up with many different stars.

Did the Hills really see a UFO? Were they examined aboard an alien spaceship? Or did the Hills have a dream they believed was real?

To this day, Betty Hill still insists that her story is true.

Lonnie Zamora

"I've got a speeder here and he won't pull over," reported Officer Lonnie Zamora to police headquarters. "I'm heading south on the highway."

"Roger. Let us know if you need backup."

Deputy Marshal Zamora worked in the small town of Socorro, New Mexico. It was April 24, 1964, at about 5:45 P.M.

As he chased the speeding car, Zamora heard a loud roar. When he turned, he saw what he described as a "flame in the sky." It was coming from a hilltop less than a mile away.

"There's a small dynamite shack over there," he thought to himself. "Maybe the whole thing blew up."

Zamora forgot about the speeding car and drove up the hill to check out the area. At the top he saw a "shiny object." It looked like an overturned car resting on four supporting legs. Next to the object stood two small people dressed in light-colored overalls. Zamora thought that one of the people seemed to notice his car.

"I may have an auto accident off the highway and am investigating on foot," he radioed headquarters. Zamora stopped the car about one hundred feet from the object. The two people were no longer in sight.

As he got out of the car and began to walk closer, Zamora heard another loud roar. Then he saw flames shooting out from underneath the object.

"Oh my gosh. It's going to explode!" he thought to himself as he turned and ran back to the car. Zamora was so frighted he bumped into the side of the vehicle, and his glasses fell off.

He took cover behind the car and saw the object lift off the ground straight up into the air about twenty-five feet. Zamora noticed some red markings on it. He also noticed that it seemed to be egg-shaped.

By now the roar was so loud that he covered his head and ducked down. Suddenly, the roar stopped and he heard a high-pitched whine, which lasted only a few seconds. As Zamora glanced up he saw the object fly over the dynamite shack and across the highway, and then disappear in the distance at a high rate of speed.

Zamora radioed for help requesting Sergeant Chavez of the State Police to come out. "Can you see a strange object or aircraft in the sky?" he asked the radio operator. The officer looked but said he saw nothing.

While waiting for Chavez to arrive, Zamora went to look around. There was burning brush in a few places and marks in the ground where the legs had rested.

When Chavez arrived, he found Zamora very pale, frightened, and sweating. Investigators were called to the scene. The Air Force sent its Project Blue Book representative, Dr. J. Allen Hynek. UFO groups and scientists were also there.

They found that three telephone calls had been received by the sheriff's office telling of a blue flaming light in the sky. This was around the time that Zamora saw the object fly away.

Investigators thought the Socorro police officer was an honest and responsible man. They believed he was telling the truth. The marks in the ground and burned areas backed up his story.

Perhaps the object was an experimental craft kept secret by the military. But there were no such crafts in the area, nor were there any helicopters, airplanes, or weather balloons.

Meanwhile, the incident was given much coverage in newspapers throughout the country. Zamora and others were interviewed over and over again.

Project Blue Book listed the Zamora sighting as unexplained, a real unidentified flying object. But not everyone believed Zamora's story.

UFO investigator Philip Klass felt that there were several unanswered questions. Mr. and Mrs. Felix Phillips lived near the spot where the UFO took off, but didn't hear the loud roar of the craft.

If there was a blast of flame when the object took off, the ground should have been burned and blackened. Yet only parts of a bush and some grass were burned.

Klass also found that the prints in the ground from the legs of the craft were slightly different from one another and different distances apart.

The town of Socorro, New Mexico, had much to gain from the Zamora UFO sighting. Tourists began stopping regularly to see the landing site, which resulted in more business for the town.

Was the whole thing just a story to get publicity and bring more tourists to the town of Socorro? Or did Lonnie Zamora really see an unidentified flying object and two small beings? If he did, who were the visitors and where did they come from?

Beverly, Massachusetts

It was 9 P.M., April 22, 1966. Eleven-year-old Nancy Modugno was in her bedroom when she saw a bright light flash through the window. She looked outside and saw an object shaped like a football flying in the air. It was the size of the family car!

Different-colored lights flashed on and off around it. They were blue, green, red, and white, and only about fifty feet away from Nancy's window. The object then flew away, toward the high school.

Nancy was scared. She ran downstairs to tell her father. He was watching television but the set suddenly lost its picture! When Nancy wouldn't calm down, her mother, Claire, and two of Claire's friends, Barbara and Brenda, told her they would go to the high school to investigate the flashing lights.

"It's probably just an airplane," said her mother. "Please don't worry about it."

The women walked to the nearby school. They saw three well-lighted flying objects circling the area. They seemed to stop in midair, then start circling again.

"It must be police or army helicopters," said Claire. "Let's get a closer look."

"That's strange," said Barbara. "They're making no noise at all."

"They can't be helicopters or airplanes," said Brenda, who watched the strange objects flash red, green, and blue lights. "They're oval-shaped."

Brenda started waving for the objects to come closer. To her surprise, one flew quietly toward her. Claire and Barbara started to run away.

"I looked up and saw a roundish object," Barbara later stated. "It was gray-white like the bottom of a plate."

Brenda stood alone in the field as it came within twenty feet of her. "I thought it might crash on my head," said Brenda. Then she, too, began to run.

The three frightened women raced back to the Modugnos' house to tell their neighbors. A group of people from the neighborhood walked down the road to watch the mysterious flying objects. One of them called the Beverly Police Department.

Officers Bossie and Mahan were sent to take a look. "I saw what seemed to be a large plate in midair over the school," Officer Mahan described later. "It had three flashing lights, red, green, and blue—but no noise."

The objects circled, picked up speed, and disappeared in the distance. That same night, a few miles away at Gordon College in Wenham, there was another sighting. Several people saw a glowing orange object fly low over the college before speeding away.

Witnesses were questioned after the Beverly incident, and an investigation was conducted. The results were published in the Condon Report. This was a study conducted by the University of Colorado on UFOs and headed by Dr. Edward Condon. The Air Force finally made the report public in January 1969.

The Condon Report stated that Bossie and Mahan actually saw the planet Jupiter that night and mistook it for a UFO.

What about the strange craft seen by the three women, eleven-year-old Nancy, and other adults in the Beverly neighborhood? Was it a real close encounter with a UFO?

The Condon Report had no explanation for the sighting by the women. It was one of twenty-three cases that could not be explained or identified.

The Nazca Drawings

Some people believe that extraterrestrials (beings from places other than Earth) visited this planet thousands of years ago. These space visitors gave prehistoric man intelligence and knowledge. This helped them develop human civilization as we know it today.

Those who support this theory point to a strange discovery in Peru. Two hundred fifty miles south of the capital city of Lima, there is a large flat area of land in the coastal desert. On the ground are thousands of lines, curves, triangles, and other shapes.

They were made by digging up the topsoil and rocks to show the lighter-colored soil underneath. Some of the lines go on for miles.

It's believed that these markings were made between 400 B.C. and A.D. 900 by the Nazca people. The lines are still easily seen because it hardly ever rains in this area.

The Nazcas were conquered by the Incas and eventually wiped out.

When airplanes began to fly over the area, it was discovered that many of the lines formed huge pictures of animals. There were enormous birds, monkeys, and spiders, which could be seen completely only from the sky. Yet these pictures were drawn by the Nazcas thousands of years before the invention of the airplane!

Why take the time to draw giant animals when none of the Nazcas could see them from the air? Who was supposed to see them?

Author Erich von Daniken believes that extraterrestrials visited the Nazcas and showed them how to draw the lines and pictures. These visitors from space used the drawings as an airfield with runways to help guide and land their spacecraft.

Many feel that the airfield theory is wrong. Why did spaceships need a runway if they landed vertically (up and down)? Why would the runways be in the shape of animals? Moreover, many of the lines run directly into hills and mountains, and the soil is too soft and sandy for a heavy craft to land on.

Von Daniken believes that the Nazcas must have had help in drawing the giant figures. Yet author Joe Nickell and his helpers reproduced the giant condor (large vulture) using only rope and stick markers. Nickell also found that many parts of the figures can be recognized from the ground.

Others believe that the lines are a huge star calendar and astronomy chart. Many mark the position of the sun at the summer and winter solstices. The solstice marks the sun's passing on June 22 to begin winter and December 22 to begin summer in the Southern Hemisphere, where Peru is located.

Perhaps the Nazcas believed that their Indian gods would look down on the giant drawings and be pleased. Or did visitors from another world use them to guide and land their spacecraft long ago?

The real reason these giant pictures were drawn still remains a mystery, one that may never be solved.

Jimmy Carter

Not all UFO sightings are reported by unknown people. Jimmy Carter, the fortieth President of the United States (1976–80), saw an unidentified flying object when he was governor of Georgia.

It happened in the town of Leary, Georgia, on January 6, 1969. It was 7:15 P.M. Governor Carter and about a dozen others were standing outside the building where he was scheduled to give a speech to the local Lions Club. When they looked up, he and the others saw a large bright object in the sky.

He filed a report with the National Investigations Committee on Aerial Phenomena (NICAP). In it, the governor said the UFO "seemed to move toward us from a distance, stopped, moved partially away, returned, and then departed."

Mr. Carter described it as "bluish at first, then reddish, luminous [shining and bright], not solid." He said it was the same size as the moon. The object seemed to be three hundred to one thousand yards away and about thirty degrees above the horizon.

This report, written in 1973, four years after the incident, listed the sighting as October 1969. But the correct date was actually January 6, 1969.

UFO investigator Robert Sheaffer studied the position of the planets on that date. He found that the planet Venus was at its brightest at that time. It was in almost the exact position the governor reported seeing the UFO.

Sheaffer believes that Governor Carter's sighting was a "misidentification of the planet Venus." He explains that sometimes Venus is so bright it can be seen in full daylight and is often mistaken for an unidentified flying object.

But Mr. Carter said it was as large as the moon. It changed colors and size as it moved closer, then farther away. It was no more than one thousand yards away.

Venus doesn't change colors or size and has no movement like that described. And the distance to the planet is thirty million miles or more!

Sheaffer believes these are incorrect descriptions of what actually happened. He states that many people are wrong in estimating distance and movements of unknown objects in the sky.

In 1978, a White House Staff assistant said that "when the President was governor of Georgia, he saw a flying object he was not able to identify."

Did Mr. Carter really see a UFO that night in 1969? Or was it the planet Venus?

Lawrence Coyne

"Captain, I see a bright red light to the east," declared crew chief Sergeant Robert Yanacsek. "Could be a warning light on top of a tower or another aircraft."

Captain Lawrence Coyne took a quick look. "Keep an eye on it," he said.

It was October 18, 1973. A United States Army Reserve helicopter left Port Columbus, Ohio, at 10:30 P.M. It was bound for its home base at Cleveland Hopkins Airport about one hundred miles away.

Captain Coyne had nineteen years of flying experience. At the controls was First Lieutenant Arrigo Jezzi. Sergeant John Healey was the flight medic.

The helicopter was flying at 2,500 feet over farmland near Mansfield, Ohio. They were about thirty minutes into the flight when Yanacsek spotted the light. The sky was clear and the weather was fair.

"The light's getting brighter, Captain," said Yanacsek. "Now it seems to be heading straight for us."

"It's coming fast now," agreed Coyne as he grabbed the controls and began a power dive of five hundred feet per minute. "It might be an F-100 jet from the Mansfield airport," he added. "Let's get out of the way."

Coyne tried calling Mansfield tower but couldn't get an answer. Then he increased the copter's dive to one thousand feet per minute and then two thousand feet per minute. But it didn't do any good. The red light was bearing down on them at a speed Coyne later estimated was more than six hundred miles per hour.

"It's no good. We're going to crash into it!" he yelled to the crew. "Brace for impact!" The copter was now at seventeen hundred feet.

Seconds passed and nothing happened. "Look up," yelled Yanacsek. "It's above us, totally stopped."

Coyne stared in amazement. "What is it?" he asked.

The four crew members saw a large gray, metallic object, fifty to sixty feet long. There was a bright red light in front and a green and white light in the back area. One of the rear lights swung around like a spotlight, flooding the cockpit in green light for two to three seconds.

Ten more seconds passed and the cigar-shaped craft turned and headed away toward the Mansfield area. Only the white light was visible now. Then it made a climbing turn to the right and disappeared over the horizon.

Coyne later estimated that the strange object was only about five hundred feet above the copter when it came to a complete stop in the air.

Coyne looked down at his instruments to find that the helicopter had climbed to 3,500 feet. Yet the controls were set for a dive.

The copter had climbed at a rate of one thousand feet per minute without power, and the crew had felt nothing.

Nor had they heard an engine sound or felt any air movement from the object that had passed so close. They only felt a small bounce when it moved away.

Did the strange gray object cause the helicopter to climb? Was it being towed up or drawn in without the crew knowing it? Was the green light some sort of power beam, or was it just a giant spotlight?

While all this was happening, Jezzi was frantically trying to contact the airport towers in the area (Mansfield, Cleveland, Columbus, and Akron), but no radio contact was made. The equipment was functioning but they couldn't transmit or receive messages. After a few minutes passed, radio contact began again. But during the incident, they had been totally cut off.

Coyne managed to bring the helicopter back down to 2,500 feet, and the flight continued on to Cleveland. After landing, he reported his sighting of an "unidentified flying object" to the Federal Aviation Administration (FAA).

Then he found out that all F-100 jets from Mansfield airport had landed *before* the incident took place. "It wasn't a jet fighter we saw," he thought to himself.

Later, Coyne described the object as having a domed area in the center. Yanacsek also thought he saw some windows along the top of the dome.

Witnesses on the ground who were traveling home in their car saw the strange object in the sky above the helicopter. They described it as "pear-shaped" or "a blimp." They also saw a light that made everything green, including the road, their car, and trees. They became very frightened. Then they saw the object move away toward Mansfield and out of sight.

UFO investigator Philip Klass believes he has the answers to the mystery. The object was a bright meteorfireball, not a UFO. He feels that it was much farther away from the helicopter than five hundred feet and that the crew members were mistaken in describing the gray, metallic surface and dome and in believing that the object had stopped.

According to Klass, the Orionids meteor showers occur at this time of year and are usually blue-green in color.

Perhaps Coyne or Jezzi pulled the copter up out of the dive without even being aware of it to avoid crashing into the ground. Radio contact was cut off simply because the helicopter was beyond the range of the airport towers.

Others state that the object was observed for too long a time for it to be a meteor-fireball. All four crew members saw and described the unknown craft. Were they and the witnesses on the ground all confused at the same time?

Could a meteor slow down to a stop and then speed up, turn, and move out of sight? Are meteor-fireballs shaped like blimps, pears, or cigars?

Was it an unidentified flying object or a meteor-fireball? There are no definite answers.

❧ II ❦

Monsters

The Giant Squid

The sea was calm on July 4, 1874. The steamer *Strathowen* was on its way to India with two hundred passengers on board. Soon after sundown, the crew noticed a small ship nearby called the *Pearl*.

It was a lovely night and many passengers were on deck enjoying the view and the good weather.

"What's that dark thing on the top of the water?" asked one man. "I didn't see that before." It was about halfway between the *Strathowen* and the *Pearl*.

"You're right," replied his wife. "It wasn't there when I looked before."

"Am I imagining things or is it moving?" he asked suddenly with fear in his voice.

As horrified eyes watched, the dark thing moved toward the *Pearl* and came up out of the water.

"It's some kind of enormous sea monster!" shouted the woman.

As the passengers on the *Strathowen* looked on, the monster crawled up over the deck of the *Pearl*. It had a huge black head and long arms, which now covered nearly one half of the helpless ship.

The *Pearl* was dragged over on its side by the creature, and the 150-ton ship disappeared in the water. Within minutes, there was no sign of the monster or the *Pearl*.

This incident was reported in the London *Times*. It was one of many eyewitness accounts of giant sea monsters that turned out to be enormous squids.

The giant squid is the largest of all invertebrates (not having a spinal column or backbone). It can shoot quickly through the water at high speeds and has ten arms with powerful suckers. Two of these arms are tentacles which can grab and trap things. The arms can hold food, which is cut into pieces by the squid's strong jaws.

Most giant squids live in the deepest part of the ocean. They usually come to the surface when they're sick or disturbed, and often at night.

The Scandinavians called these giant creatures *kraken*. They were believed to be mythological monsters that didn't really exist. But several huge dead squids washed up on beaches, and scientists were able to examine the remains. One was over fifty-five feet long!

Scientists never thought squids could grow to such large sizes. In fact, they're not really sure how big these creatures can actually grow.

The giant squid and another huge animal, the sperm whale, are enemies. Whales eat squids and the two often fight to the death. Whales are sometimes found with sucker marks on their bodies from fights with squids.

Scientists believe that the length through the center of the squid's suckers is about 1/100 of the squid's total size. One report described a sucker mark on a sperm whale eighteen inches across. This would mean that the head and body of the squid measured 150 feet. The arms and tentacles stretch much longer than the body, so the total length of this huge creature would be more than 600 feet!

Others have found sucker marks on whales that fought with squids eighty feet long. But many scientists are not willing to accept that squids grow to this size without having actual remains to examine.

There have been many accounts of giant squids attacking people and ships. In 1802, a hungry squid snatched two men off a platform on the side of a ship. One of its arms was chopped off by crew members and it was nearly forty feet long!

In 1941, survivors of a ship that had been sunk were floating on a raft in the Atlantic Ocean. They were attacked by a giant squid and one man was captured and taken away by the creature.

Another giant squid attacked a sailing ship and threw its arms around the masts. The weight of the squid nearly toppled the ship over in the water. But the crew managed to cut off the arms of the creature with axes and knives.

Still another squid attached itself to a ship and actually swallowed the mast, complete with sails and rigging. With a full stomach, the giant creature returned to the water and disappeared.

The giant squid is a monster that really exists. But for many years the stories about them were believed to be just tall tales or the result of overactive imaginations.

How big can they get? No one knows for sure. But if there really is a giant squid six hundred feet long, its body and arms would stretch as long as two football fields placed end to end!

The Loch Ness Monster

For years people talked about seeing strange things in the loch (lake). Most of the local residents had heard tales of the large, frightening "monster" who lived in the deep, dark waters of Loch Ness.

Arthur Grant had heard the stories, too. His parents' home was in Drumnadrochit, Scotland, on the northern shore of Loch Ness.

It was January 5, 1934. Grant was on vacation from medical school and riding home on his motorcycle from the town of Inverness. It was 1 A.M. and the road was deserted.

The night was cloudy but the sky cleared for a moment and the moon lit up the area.

"What's that up ahead?" Grant asked himself. He saw a large dark thing in the distance on the side of the road.

As he slowed down the motorcycle, Grant was shocked

to see the thing start to move. "It's alive," he thought. He watched it go across the road into the bushes.

Grant followed the mysterious creature on foot and saw it jump into the loch and disappear under the water. "I've seen it," he thought. "I've seen the Loch Ness Monster!"

Later, he said, "It had a long neck and large eyes with a small head." Grant described a body with two humps and a long tail, which was rounded at the end. The thing was about fifteen to twenty feet long and dark black or brown in color.

Then Grant drew a picture of what he had seen. His drawing showed four flipper-type legs. The next day, flipper prints were found on the beach.

Arthur Grant was one of thousands of people over the last fourteen hundred years to have claimed to see the Loch Ness Monster, either in the water or on land.

Loch Ness is a deep, cold lake in the northern part of Scotland. It is the largest body of fresh water in the British Isles. The lock is twenty-four and a half miles long, but its average width is only a mile. The deepest part is 920 feet, but most of the loch is an average of 500 feet deep.

The temperature is a cold forty-two degrees all year round. The water doesn't freeze in the winter and never warms up in the summer. It's so brown and murky that visibility is only a few feet. Few people swim in the dark water and divers can't see clearly. When something falls to the bottom, it never comes back up because of the strong loch undercurrents.

Dr. Roy Mackal of the University of Chicago chose 251 of the most detailed sightings of the Loch Ness Monster from among thousands of reports. After studying them carefully, he found that the sightings didn't happen at any special time of the day, month, or year. They occurred in all areas of the loch and most lasted for only a few minutes.

He did find that many sightings happened on calm, sunny days. The head of the monster was often described as vertical—straight up and down in the water. The body length was about twenty to twenty-five feet. The creature's movements in the water were zigzag, with fast changes of direction and bursts of speed. On land, it moved more slowly.

Photographs and motion pictures have been taken of the Loch Ness Monster over the years. But the quality of the film hasn't been good and the distance was too great for any definite identification. After studying these photos and movies, Dr. Mackal stated that the "monster" is real— some type of water animal that occasionally comes to the surface of the loch.

Sonar detection has also been used to identify the Loch Ness Monster. Sonar is like radar but it uses sound pulses directed through the water. Sonar can detect objects in the water as well as their direction, depth, and range.

Sonar studies in the late 1960s showed that large objects *are* swimming in Loch Ness. They're moving as fast as seventeen miles per hour and diving at speeds of five miles per hour. These objects live on the bottom or sides of the loch.

But what are these large objects? Mackal believes that they are a *group* of fish-eating water animals that live in the loch, not a single creature. He thinks they have an amphibious quality that lets them move on land awkwardly but travel quickly in the water. Their limbs are like flippers and they have powerful tails.

Mackal stated, "Whatever the identity of the animals in Loch Ness, they do exist!"

There are many other theories about the Loch Ness Monster. Some believe the creature is related to the plesiosaurs, a group of large water reptiles. But plesiosaurs are cold-blooded, with no inner body temperature controls. The waters of the loch would be too cold for reptiles.

Could the monster be a giant sea slug, a twenty-foot version of a snail without a shell, even though the largest known sea slug is only a little more than a foot long?

The Loch Ness Monster has been described over the years as a giant worm, a long-necked otter, a sea cow, a swimming elephant, and a giant eel.

There are some who believe the monster in the loch doesn't exist at all. They feel that the sightings are the result of active imaginations. They think that many people saw floating logs, tires, birds, or waves in the loch and mistook them for the creature.

Until a living animal is captured or a dead body is examined, the Loch Ness Monster will be a creature of mystery. When detailed photos or films are taken that clearly show the identity of the animal, then people will believe there really is a Loch Ness Monster.

Until then, all we do know is that there's something strange in the loch!

The Yeti (Abominable Snowman)

"Look at these giant footprints," declared mountain climber Eric Shipton to his friend Michael Ward. Their guide, Sen Tensing, wasn't at all surprised to see the prints in the snow.

"They're Yeti tracks," he said confidently.

Shipton and Ward were exploring an area in the Himalayas, 18,000 feet above sea level. The Himalayas are the tallest mountains on earth. Mount Everest, the highest peak in the world (29,028 feet), is located there.

This great mountain range extends through the small countries of Tibet, Nepal, Sikkim, and Bhutan. It is this area that is the home of the Yetis. They're also called "abominable snowmen," a name given by a newspaper reporter in 1921.

It was four o'clock in the afternoon of November 8,

1951, when Shipton and Ward made their discovery. They, too, had heard the stories about the Yeti.

"These look like fresh tracks," stated Shipton. "Let's follow them."

After about a mile, the men lost sight of the tracks but decided to take photographs of their find. Shipton took a few pictures of the sharpest of the strange prints. One shot showed Ward's boot next to the footprint. Another was of Ward's axe next to the print in the snow.

The footprints were very clear. They appeared to be 13 by 8 inches, longer and much wider than the foot of a human. The British Museum said they were the prints of a langur monkey. But this was incorrect, since a langur's foot is no larger than 8 by 2 inches.

Others tried to explain away the photo by saying that melting ice can enlarge normal footprints. That's why they were so big. But a melting print is easy to spot. The toe marks melt onto each other and are not distinct and separate, as they were in Shipton's pictures. In fact, Shipton's print clearly showed a very long second toe.

Anthropologist John Napier thinks that it could have been a double print, one on top of the other. But he's not sure what made it. His guess is that it was a human foot without shoes walking over the track of a foot wearing a moccasin.

Do Yetis exist? The Sherpas, a tribe in Nepal, believe the Yeti (which means "wild man") is real and not just part of their mythology. They say there are two types of Yetis. The large ones are called *dzu-teh* and the small ones are called *meh-teh*.

Their height can be anywhere from four and a half feet to a giant sixteen feet. The hair is red-brown, dark brown, or black, and covers the entire body.

The arms of a Yeti are long. Although Yetis walk on

two feet, they're hunched over. They are very strong and muscular creatures. Some Sherpas have described their skulls as cone-shaped, and some say their feet point backward.

But Sherpas aren't the only ones who have seen Yetis or found footprints. The Chinese and Russians have also reported sightings of strange upright hairy creatures.

The first sighting by a Westerner was in 1820. There were other sightings in 1832, 1906, and 1915. In 1921, a British officer spotted a group of dark, upright creatures from a distance. He explored the area and found large nonhuman footprints in the snow.

His guides described the creatures that made these prints as "wild men of the snow." But when the officer wrote up his report of this unusual discovery, he accidentally wrote the native word for "bad-smelling man of the snow." This was then interpreted as "abominable snowman." A reporter used the name, and soon newspapers throughout the world were writing about "the abominable snowman of the Himalayas." Most people treated the whole incident as a joke, but the name stuck.

Sightings of strange hairy men continued. In the 1950s several expeditions traveled to the Himalayas to find Yetis. More footprints were found and photographed, but no Yeti was seen.

One expedition brought back Yeti hair, which couldn't be identified. It was similar to both human and ape hair but not exactly like either. Other Yeti scalps were found to be fakes when examined by scientists.

In 1972, zoologist E. W. Cronin, Jr., and Dr. Howard Emery took photos of what they believed were Yeti footprints made during the night in their camp. The sun hadn't risen yet, so no melting had taken place. The footprints measured 9 by 4¾ inches and looked very much like Shipton's 1951 prints, including the large second toe.

Cronin and Emery were careful to examine and photograph all other tracks they saw as a basis for comparison. They also found that the sun and wind had no effect on their own footprints even after one day.

Both men concluded that the prints were real and unchanged. They were not made by any *known* animal today but by an unidentified living creature.

Other interesting prints that are very much alike have been discovered in different areas. Footprints found in 1978 by Lord John Hunt in the Himalayas (which measure 13¾ by 6¾ inches) closely match prints found by a Russian expedition in the Pamirs mountains in 1979. The Pamirs prints measure 13¼ by 6¼ inches.

There are some who believe that the Yetis don't exist. Until a live or dead specimen is examined by knowledgeable scientists, these people will continue to disbelieve reported sightings and photographs of footprints.

Others feel that the many sightings and prints have been so similar to each other over the years that the Yetis' existence cannot be denied.

If they do exist, what are they? There are several theories. Some believe that the Yetis are relatives of *Gigantopithecus*, the now extinct giant apes. These large apes lived millions of years ago in southern Asia. But there's no evidence that they walked upright on two feet like the Yetis.

Others say they are related to the more manlike *Paranthropus*, which walked on two feet as well as on all four feet. Some look to Neanderthal man as the relative of the Yeti. But many feel that the Neanderthals were too advanced. They built fires, used stone tools, and buried their dead.

Are Yetis real? Scientists won't believe it until they have skeletal evidence.

Were the hundreds of sightings and footprints imagined, or were they cases of mistaken identity? Many are convinced that the Yeti is a living creature. But no one can prove it.

The Komodo Dragon

The huge monster sensed that food was close. Its forked yellow tongue moved in and out of its mouth. It began to stalk a wild pig that had wandered nearby.

The leathery skin, heavy body, and long powerful tail made the dragonlike creature appear even more dangerous and frightening. Moving as fast as twelve miles per hour, the ten-foot-long monster, weighing over three hundred pounds, caught its prey.

The sharp deadly claws and sharklike teeth ripped the pig apart. Finally, the beast swallowed the back end of the dead animal in one large gulp. Then off it went among the rocks to lie still and digest its meal.

Did this scene take place millions of years ago in the age of dinosaurs? Is it part of an old horror movie about prehistoric monsters?

The answer is no! This monster is alive and living today,

a relative of the "terrible lizards" (dinosaurs) of the past. It's called the Komodo Dragon.

These creatures live on Komodo Island and other small Indonesian islands in the South Pacific. Since the island of Komodo had not been inhabited by people, the creatures weren't discovered officially until 1912. They were put under government protection and are safe from hunters. Except for being unable to breathe fire, they look very much like the dragons of mythology and legends. They live for up to one hundred years.

The Komodo Dragon is actually a type of monitor lizard which can be as small as eight inches. Although the average Komodo Dragon is ten feet long, sightings of specimens much larger have been recorded. There have been reports of twenty-three-foot-long dragons weighing nearly one thousand pounds!

This type of lizard has a head that can turn in every direction. It can enlarge its mouth in order to swallow large animals. It uses its powerful tail, teeth, and claws as weapons.

The Komodo Dragon eats live or dead animals and other lizards, too. A full-grown adult will attack hogs, goats, deer, and even water buffaloes.

These creatures are very good swimmers. They'll swim through heavy currents of water to attack other animals.

When the Dragons decide to take a mate, the males stand up on their back legs and try to push each other over. The lizard left standing wins the female as its partner.

After mating, the dragons lay eggs. When hatched, the baby dragon is only eighteen inches long. It lives its first year of life in the trees.

As frightening as a full-grown Komodo Dragon looks, it doesn't roar, growl, or snort. It barely makes any sound at all, even when it's attacking other animals or tearing them apart.

If a huge and frightening Komodo Dragon can attack and eat a water buffalo, it can do the same to people. Natives of Komodo Island and visitors are very much afraid of these dangerous creatures and avoid them.

Legend becomes reality on Komodo Island. The dragons of childhood fairy tales and the creatures of prehistoric times come together to form a real-life monster that exists today.

Mothman

"There's something moving near the power plant," Roger Scarberry said to his wife, Linda.

"It's some kind of giant bird with wings," added their friend Steve Mallette.

"I can see its eyes from here," said Mary, Steve's wife. "They're red and glowing." She turned to her husband. "I'm afraid, Steve."

"Let's get out of here and fast!"

The two young married couples were taking a drive together on the night of November 17, 1966. They were riding through the now deserted ordnance works, which had been a World War II weapons factory. It was located about seven miles outside of Point Pleasant, West Virginia.

The place was known as the TNT area. It was a favorite spot for teenagers and people who wanted to be alone.

They drove quickly toward town. As the car rounded a

sharp curve, they saw the creature again on the hillside near the road.

"There it is again!" yelled Roger. "I thought we left it far behind."

"It looks like a large man," said Linda.

"I never saw a man with wings!" Steve declared.

"Look!" shouted Mary. "It's spreading them. They're huge."

But instead of flying away like a bird, the strange winged creature shot straight up into the air like a helicopter at great speed.

"That thing gives me the creeps," said Roger. "Let's get out of here." He drove as fast as he could toward town.

"How did it fly straight up like that?" asked Steve. "That's unbelievable. It didn't even flap its wings."

"We haven't lost it yet. It's flying right above us. Listen," whispered Mary.

They all heard a strange noise on the roof of the car and were terrified.

"I can't go any faster," explained Roger. "I'm hitting a hundred miles per hour already."

The creature swooped down above them and made loud squealing sounds. They could see its eerie shadow cast by the moonlight on the side of the road. It was still directly above the car, traveling just as fast as they were driving.

As they reached the outskirts of the town, the frightening creature finally flew away. The Scarberrys and Mallettes drove right to the police station to report what had happened to them.

The next morning the police investigated the TNT area but found nothing to back up their story. But the officers did report some unusual radio interference.

The four held a press conference and the story received national attention. The strange creature was described as birdlike. One reporter used the name Mothman in his story, and others picked it up.

A week later, a shoe store manager spotted Mothman north of Point Pleasant. Other sightings were reported. An eighteen-year-old girl got a close look at Mothman's face. He had "fiery, red eyes."

"It was horrible," she said. "Like something out of a science fiction movie." The girl claimed that her own eyes burned for days after staring into the monster's face.

There were dozens of reported sightings of Mothman and any number of unreported ones. Many people kept it to themselves because they didn't want to be ridiculed by other people or the press.

The Mothman sightings were similar in several ways. They all described a creature six to seven feet tall, gray-white or gray-brown in color with wings that stretched ten or more feet when fully extended. Its eyes were big and red and it could fly at very high speeds.

There were reports of radio and television interference and even trouble starting cars in the areas where Mothman was seen. These things are usually connected to UFO sightings. As a result, many people began to believe that Mothman was actually an extraterrestrial or monster from space.

What was this strange birdlike creature? One biologist stated it was really a sandhill crane, which stands as tall as a person and is gray in color. It has large, bright red rings around its eyes. The only problem was that this type of crane spends the winter in warm climates, usually west of the Mississippi or in Florida.

Most police and wildlife officials did not take the Mothman sightings seriously. They believed they were exaggerated accounts by very frightened people.

The following year, on December 16, 1967, the Silver

Bridge near Point Pleasant collapsed. Cars slid into the Ohio River, killing nearly forty people.

Some believed that Mothman was responsible for this tragedy. They felt that the birdlike monster was a sign of evil. Others were sure Mothman was a creature from space and arrived here in a UFO. But many believed that the Mothman sightings were simply the result of overactive imaginations.

A sign of evil, UFO, or imagination? Without proof, the truth about Mothman will never be known for sure.

Ogopogo (Naitaka)

The *New York Times* newspaper once offered one thousand dollars to anyone who could bring them a photograph of the lake monster, Ogopogo.

The citizens of Kelowna, in British Columbia, Canada, have built a statue of Ogopogo in the city park. It's the first one ever constructed for a monster. They also made the creature an honorary citizen.

Ogopogo lives in Okanagan Lake, Canada. The lake is sixty-nine miles long, one to two and a half miles wide, and about two thousand feet deep. The local Sushwap Indians have always believed that a giant water creature lives in the lake. They call it Naitaka.

There are Indian drawings of Naitaka on the nearby cliffs overlooking the lake. They show a creature with a head like a goat with two bumps on the top. It has a long neck, a thick snake's body, flippers, and a short tail.

One Indian legend tells of a visiting chief named Timbasket:

"The most dangerous part of the lake is Monster's Island," explained the Sushwap medicine man to their visitor, Chief Timbasket. "Naitaka lives nearby in a large cave. Don't paddle your canoe there."

"I don't believe in your monster spirit of the lake," replied Chief Timbasket. "I'm taking my family on a canoe ride and have no fear of this creature."

"Please take a gift along for the monster to eat—a dog, a duck, a chicken, or a piece of deer. All of the Sushwap do this and it keeps our people safe."

"There is no monster," declared Timbasket. "I am chief and I'm not afraid."

The medicine man placed a dog in the canoe.

"Push the dog overboard and no harm will come your way," he yelled as the chief paddled off into the lake. "Stay away from Monster's Island and the cave," he shouted from shore.

The chief turned to his family and said, "He's acting like an old woman. I won't drown a dog because the Sushwap are afraid."

Chief Timbasket stayed close to shore and headed directly toward Monster's Island. The Sushwap on shore watched in horror. "Give the spirit his gift," the medicine man shouted. But the dog remained aboard the canoe.

As the small craft passed near the cave and island, the water on the lake suddenly started to churn and foam.

"Naitaka is angered," whispered the medicine man. "The chief is doomed."

Waves that weren't there seconds before crashed against the rocks and shore. The spray from the waves was everywhere. But moments later, it was over. The lake was calm again.

The Sushwap on shore saw the chief's canoe. It was

overturned and floating in the lake. He and his family had disappeared.

"The monster has taken his revenge," said the medicine man sadly.

Stories like this one became common knowledge around the area. The early Canadian settlers believed them, too. They routinely traveled across the lake with a small animal that they dropped overboard as a gift to Naitaka.

In the 1850s, two separate incidents happened involving men crossing the lake with their horses. The men were saved, but the horses were pulled down under the water by a mysterious force. Both men had forgotten their small gifts for Naitaka. Perhaps the horses were taken instead.

The sightings continued over the years. Mrs. John Allison saw a strange humped monster in 1852. One man described it as a "telegraph pole with a sheep's head." Others said it was thirty feet long with five humps and a forked tail. One woman said it was "a big, snakelike creature." Still another described it as a "prehistoric monster twenty feet long with a heavy, snakelike body."

Something strange lived in Okanagan Lake. A clue as to what it was may have washed up on shore in 1914. The dead body of a mysterious animal was found on one of the beaches. It was about six feet long and weighed four hundred pounds. It had a round head with two tusks, flippers with claws, and a wide tail.

Some said it was a sea cow, or manatee. But these tropical animals live in the West Indies and South America. If it wasn't a sea cow, then what was it? Some say it might have been some sort of a baby monster. No one will ever know, since the remains were never studied by scientists.

In the 1920s, the lake monster got a new name. A British song-and-dance man sang about a creature named Ogopogo, and the name has stuck ever since:

His mother was an insect
His father was a whale
A little bit of head
And hardly any tail
And Ogopogo was his name.

Since the 1950s, there have been many sightings of Ogopogo. Individuals have seen the monster from shore. Once a whole group of tourists in a bus saw the monster.

One of the clearest accounts was by Richard Miller, a local publisher. It happened on July 20, 1959. The whole Miller family saw Ogopogo while they were on their boat on the lake. The monster was only 250 feet away and they watched it for three minutes before it went under the water.

"The head was definitely snakelike with a blunt nose," said Miller. He went on to describe five humps and skin. Miller estimated that the creature was gliding along at fifteen to seventeen miles per hour.

Is Ogopogo a relative of the Loch Ness Monster thousands of miles away? Descriptions of the creatures are very much alike. But there have been no clear photographs or films of Ogopogo.

Scientists haven't shown interest in Okanagan Lake like they have at Loch Ness. Perhaps a scientific investigation would shed more light on these similarities.

Does Ogopogo really exist? Many respected people who have seen this mysterious creature think so.

But without more proof, such as a living or dead specimen, there will always be those who doubt its existence.

Bigfoot (Sasquatch)

A large creature suddenly appeared from behind a group of small trees and shrubs. It moved quickly out into the open and then it headed toward the thick forest. The thing was seven to eight feet tall and weighed several hundred pounds.

At first glance it looked like a giant man walking upright on two feet. But it was dark brown in color and the body was totally covered with hair.

It had a short neck, long arms, and huge, powerful-looking shoulders. Seconds later, the creature disappeared into the trees.

This is an example of one of the more than one thousand sightings of Bigfoot in North America. It happened on June 6, 1978, at 8 A.M. Two senior survey engineers named Kendall and Hathaway were about to start work in the northern Cascade Range in the state of Washington. They were at four thousand feet and had just left their truck. It was a cold, clear morning.

The creature was in view for only a few seconds but at very close range. The men immediately searched the place where it had disappeared. They found no footprints, since the ground was very hard.

For years, Kendall and Hathaway had heard the Bigfoot stories. But they never took them seriously, not until they saw one with their own eyes.

Canadians use the Salish Indian word *sasquatch* to describe the mysterious "wild man of the woods." In the United States (mainly in Oregon, Washington, and Northern California), the creature is called Bigfoot, from the Hupa Indian word *oh-mah*.

Does Bigfoot exist? Many people think so. There's a Bigfoot Information Center at Hood River, Oregon. A carving of the creature from a redwood tree is on display in Willow Creek, California. In 1969, a county in Oregon passed a law forbidding the killing of a Bigfoot. A fine of $10,000 and/or prison for up to five years is the punishment.

Of the many sightings and footprints discovered over the years, only a small number are considered by experts to be reliable. That is, they are not a hoax or fake and they're not identified as a large animal such as a bear.

Most of the footprints discovered measured between 12 and 24 inches long, with the average about 16 by 7 inches. A set of 1,089 Bigfoot tracks was found near Bossburg, Washington, in October 1969. The left print was very large—17½ by 7 inches. The right print was of a crippled foot, called a clubfoot.

A clubfoot is misshapen and twisted out of position usually from birth or after a severe injury. Some experts who have studied the Bossberg prints feel that the clubfoot was the result of an injury to the creature and would be very difficult to fake.

In the early 1970s, a man named Alan Berry recorded the voice of a Bigfoot on tape. He was in the High Sierra Nevada Mountains in Northern California at the 8,500-foot level. The unusual sounds on the tape were studied carefully by voice and sound experts. The range, pitch, and strength of the sounds were measured.

The experts concluded that the living creature that made the sounds had a voice box much larger than a normal human being's and was about eight feet tall. The sound experts believed the tape was real, not a fake.

A movie film of a Bigfoot was taken in October 1967 by Roger Patterson and Bob Gimlin. But many still disagree to this day whether the film is real or a hoax.

Both men were on horseback in Northern California searching for Bigfoot. As they rounded a curve in a creek, the horses became afraid and reared up on their back legs. Both men were thrown from their horses but were not hurt.

Then Patterson saw the large creature that had frightened the horses. He grabbed his movie camera, which was already loaded with film just in case something like this happened.

Patterson began filming and running toward the creature. The result was twenty feet of sometimes blurry color film of a female Bigfoot about seven feet tall and 350 pounds. At one point, the creature even turned and looked toward Patterson, who was about a hundred feet away.

The big question remains, was the film part of a hoax or was it real? Was it an actor in a gorilla suit or was it Bigfoot? Scientists who viewed the film were undecided.

Some people felt that the creature's body movements were exaggerated. The footprints of the Patterson Bigfoot were 14 by 5 inches. Scientists calculated that it was 7 feet

8 inches to 8 feet 3 inches tall. But the length between steps (the stride) was only forty-one inches. An eight-foot creature would normally have a stride of fifty-six inches. Was it really a normal-size man in the film trying to take big, exaggerated steps?

Bigfoot?

Patterson's camera was set for either sixteen or twenty-four frames per second. He can't remember which, because of all the excitement!

Dr. Don Grieve of the Royal Free Hospital School of Medicine in London analyzed the film carefully. He measured stride length, leg swing, and speed of walking. Since the speed of the film was unknown, Grieve had several conclusions.

If the film was taken at sixteen or eighteen frames per second, a regular human being *could not* copy the walk of the Bigfoot. If the film was taken at twenty-four frames per second or faster, it would be possible for a tall man to copy the walk.

Does Bigfoot exist? There's no hard physical evidence to support that it does. Scientists need skeletons or living or dead specimens as conclusive evidence.

The many sightings, footprints, and voice recording do not prove, *beyond a doubt,* that Bigfoot is real. But many believe that there *is* something out there that cannot be easily explained. If the creature didn't exist, why are there still so many sightings and reports of footprints year after year?

Psychologists and others explain this by saying that people *want* Bigfoot to exist. They want to believe there are still mysteries in the world that remain unanswered.

If Bigfoot is real, what kind of a creature is it? Like the Yeti (Abominable Snowman) in Asia, some believe that Bigfoot is a relative or form of the giant ape called *Gigantopithecus,* which is now extinct. Others say that these are a form of prehistoric man like *Paranthropus* or Neander-thal.

Until there is hard physical evidence, the scientific world will not believe in the existence of Bigfoot. But those who have seen or heard the creature are convinced that it is real.

❧ III ❧

ESP
and Other
Mysteries

The Nightmare Crash

"Something's wrong with that plane's engines," said David Booth as he looked up at the sky.

The huge American Airlines jetliner turned suddenly and rolled over in the air. Then, as David watched in horror, it crashed to the ground, exploding in flames.

He felt the heat of the fire and screamed out loud. When he opened his eyes, David saw that he was in his own bed.

"What a horrible dream!" thought the terrified twenty-three-year-old. All day long, the young office manager from Cincinnati, Ohio, couldn't stop thinking about his nightmare.

"It wasn't like a dream," said David. "It was like I was standing there watching the whole thing—like watching television."

For ten nights in a row, David Booth had the same horrible nightmare. ''There was never any doubt to me that something was going to happen,'' he said.

Finally, sick with worry, David felt he had to tell someone about the dreams. He called American Airlines and a psychiatrist at the nearby university. They listened but could do nothing. On May 22, 1979, he called the Federal Aviation Administration (FAA) at the Cincinnati airport.

The FAA tried to gather facts from David's dream. It was an American Airlines plane, and very likely a DC-10. But where or when the crash might occur was impossible to tell.

Three days later, on May 25, 1979, David Booth sat in front of his television set. He listened in shock as a newscaster described the worst air disaster in United States history.

American Airlines Flight 191 had just taken off from Chicago's O'Hare International Airport headed for Los Angeles. The DC-10 rose to the northwest just after 3 P.M.

''The plane lost power and slowly rolled over on its side,'' said one eyewitness to the *New York Times*. He then described a ''huge ball of fire'' as it crashed.

''The left engine was smoking badly on takeoff,'' said another witness. There was a burst of flame and the engine fell. Then the plane swung over to the left and plunged to the ground.''

Flames from the crash shot 125 feet into the air. All 272 people on board were killed in addition to three on the ground.

''It was uncanny,'' said Jack Barker of the FAA. ''The greatest similarity was his calling the airline American and the airplane DC-10 . . . and that the plane came in inverted [upside down].''

Extrasensory perception (ESP) researchers believed David had a precognitive dream. He had a vision of the future. The knowledge came to him from other than the five basic senses.

David Booth stopped having nightmares after the crash, but he's still upset by the experience. "There's no explanation for it," he declared. "It just doesn't make sense."

Was it extrasensory perception or a terrible coincidence?

The Story of Chris

Chris did card tricks and difficult math problems for friends of the family.

He appeared on television and on the stage. He was even a guest speaker once.

There's no doubt that Chris was a talented ten-year-old.

He was also a dog—a dark tan, mixed-breed beagle.

Chris lived with Mr. and Mrs. George Wood of Greenwich, Rhode Island, in the 1950s. He was a year old when he joined the Wood family. Mrs. Wood was an artist and Mr. Wood was a chemist. They had no children.

When Chris was five, a guest brought a dog to the house that could spell its name by pawing out numbers for letters. For example, 1 was A, 2 was B, etc. The dog could also do simple math problems.

Just for fun, Chris, who had watched the other dog, was asked, "How much is two and two?" To Mrs. Wood's surprise, Chris pawed her arm four times.

Within days, Chris pawed out 1 to 10 and did simple arithmetic. In months, he was able to solve more difficult problems. Mr. Wood even brought some engineers to the house to prove that his dog could do math.

Soon Chris knew the alphabet and gave correct answers to questions when neither of the Woods knew the answers. He spelled out the letters by using the number code with his paw.

Reporters interviewed Chris and wrote about him in newspapers. He appeared with Garry Moore on his popular 1950s TV show. Any fees Chris earned were given to charity, such as the Society for the Prevention of Cruelty to Animals (SPCA).

Once Chris told a friend of the family which horses would win the daily double at a nearby racetrack. He pawed the post position numbers of the horses on her arm after she asked him.

The woman bet two dollars and won eighty-four. Surprised and amazed, she called in professors from Rhode Island College and the Parapsychology Lab at Duke University to run tests on Chris.

He was tested hundreds of times with the Zener cards, the main test for ESP. There were twenty-five cards in all, five each of circles, crosses, wavy lines, squares, and stars.

One person would look at a card. Chris, in a different part of the house, would identify the symbol on the card by pawing on a second person's arm.

The cards were always packed in a special order in a closed box by the researchers. The two helpers used in the experiments would switch places every so often and start at different parts of the deck each time. They did this to prove there was no trickery and that they weren't giving Chris the answers or answering for him.

Although he didn't do as well when tested by strangers, his scores were always extremely high. In one set of tests,

Chris had a score that could happen by chance only once in a hundred billion times!

For the most part, he lived the life of any ordinary dog. He ran through the neighborhood with his German shepherd friend and never tired of chasing cars.

Chris's scores have never been equaled by any other dog. His test results come closest to proving that there really is ESP in animals.

But Chris wasn't always 100 percent right. He was one day off in predicting his own death.

Dream of Death

President Abraham Lincoln was asleep in the White House and dreaming. It was April 1865. The War Between the States, after four years of bloody fighting, had ended on April 9. General Robert E. Lee of the Southern Confederacy surrendered his army to Northern General Ulysses S. Grant at Appomattox Courthouse, Virginia.

Suddenly, Lincoln opened his eyes. "It's too quiet in the White House," he thought. Then he heard someone crying. Could it be his wife, Mary, in the next room? The President got out of bed to look, but Mary wasn't there.

He walked into the hall and saw no one. Where were the security guards? Even his secretary's room was empty.

"Where is everyone?" thought Lincoln.

He walked downstairs and found that the East Room was full of people. Lincoln saw a structure covered in black velvet in the center of the room. On the velvet lay a body wrapped in a sheet. Its face was completely covered.

Soldiers stood guard throughout the room. People walked past the body. Some were crying. Others stared in shock.

"What's going on here?" thought Lincoln.

He walked up to one of the nearest soldiers and asked, "Who is dead in the White House?"

Without looking at Lincoln, the soldier declared, "The President. He was murdered by an assassin."

Just then a woman screamed loudly, and Lincoln sat up straight in his bed. He was covered in sweat.

"A dream, it was just a dream!" he said to himself. "Was I the one who was dead at the White House, or does it mean something else?" He spent the rest of the night wide awake and wondering.

Lincoln was upset by the dream. He told it to his wife and friends. Death threats had been made against him throughout his presidency. Lincoln often felt he wouldn't have long to live after the Civil War ended.

Soon it was April 14, 1865. The President and his wife attended a stage performance of the play *Our American Cousin* at Ford's Theater in Washington.

Shortly after 10 P.M. John Wilkes Booth entered the Presidential Box at the theater and stood five feet away from Lincoln. He shot the President once in the back of the head with a small pistol.

The next morning, the sixty-one-year-old sixteenth President of the United States was dead of an assassin's bullet. His body was taken to the East Room of the White House.

Was it extrasensory perception? Did he have a vision of the future called precognition?

Or was Lincoln's dream the result of his worrying about death threats he received during his presidency? Perhaps it was just an unfortunate coincidence.

Whatever it was, Abraham Lincoln's dream came true.

Innocent or Guilty?

"I swear that I'm innocent!" shouted the young man to the jury. "I didn't kill him."

It was 1894 and Will Purvis had just been tried and convicted of the murder of a farmer in Columbia, Mississippi.

"We the jurors declare Will Purvis guilty of murder in the first degree!"

Purvis was shocked. He shook his head slowly.

"I don't believe it," he mumbled. "I'm innocent. I swear I didn't do it."

When he was sentenced to death by hanging, Purvis cried out loudly to the jury, "I'll live to see every last one of you die." As they took him back to jail in handcuffs, he yelled, "I'll outlive all of you!"

On February 7, 1894, Will Purvis was taken from his jail cell to the gallows. A crowd of three thousand people had gathered to watch the execution. Purvis, who still insisted he was innocent, stood above the trapdoor of the platform.

The sheriff placed the noose around his neck. The crowd held its breath. The deputy released the trapdoor which opened beneath Purvis's feet. He plunged to his death—or so everyone thought.

"There he is," shouted some people in the crowd. "He's still alive!"

The noose had come undone and slipped over his head. Will Purvis walked out from under the gallows very much alive.

"The sentence will be carried out," said the sheriff as deputies led him back up the steps of the platform. The noose was tied again and put around his neck.

"It's a miracle!" the crowd shouted. Let him live!"

Three thousand people insisted that Purvis be spared from death. Knowing he would have an ugly mob scene on his hands if he opposed them, Sheriff Irvin Magee led Purvis back to his cell.

Although his lawyers appealed, a new date of execution was set for December 12, 1895. But before the sentence could be carried out, Purvis's friends rescued him from jail and he went into hiding.

A few weeks later, a new governor was elected in Mississippi. Purvis gave himself up and the new governor listened to his claims of innocence and believed him. On March 12, 1896, the governor changed his sentence to life in prison.

The story was reported in detail by Mississippi newspapers, and Purvis became famous throughout the state. Thousands of people wrote letters to the governor asking him to grant a full pardon and free the young prisoner.

Finally, in 1898, the governor pardoned Purvis and he became a free man. Nineteen years later, Joseph Beard confessed on his deathbed that it was he, not Will Purvis, who had murdered the farmer.

Purvis's name was finally cleared, and in 1920, the state of Mississippi gave him a check for $5,000 as a form of payment for his years in prison.

His life had been spared when the noose slipped. Some say it was because the rope was made of a wiry grass that couldn't keep the knot tied. Others believe the noose had been greased. But many claim it was a miracle—that a higher power saved the life of an innocent man.

Purvis shouted to the jury in 1894 that he'd live longer than all of them. It was a declaration that came true years later.

On October 13, 1938, three days after the death of the last juror, Will Purvis died. He outlived every one of them!

Changing the Future

Mrs. Dodd (not her real name) was a happy woman. The next day she would be seeing her husband for the first time in three months.

Mr. Dodd was chief engineer for a steamship company during World War I. Even commercial vessels were in danger of being fired on by warships from other countries. Mrs. Dodd was relieved that her husband was coming home safe and sound.

Although she lived in California, Mrs. Dodd traveled to Philadelphia to meet her husband. She was told by the steamship company that he'd be arriving at Pier 101 the next morning around four.

That night she went to bed early and had a strange and disturbing dream.

"I dreamed that the ship came in, unloaded its cargo, and then sailed immediately for India without my knowledge," she later explained. "Thirty hours from port, a torpedo hit the ship. It sank and my husband was the only one hurt.''

Mrs. Dodd woke up at 3:40 A.M., dressed quickly, and took a taxi to Pier 101. She ran past the guard at the gate onto the ship and into the arms of her husband, who was on deck.

"Don't go. Please don't go. The ship is going down," she cried. "I had a dream that was so real!" she explained. "The ship will be hit by a torpedo and sink and you'll be hurt."

Mr. Dodd tried to calm his wife down, wondering how she knew the ship was bound for India. His wife was so determined to get him off that he finally asked permission to be excused from the voyage. Permission was granted and the Dodds headed for home.

Three weeks later, Mr. Dodd reported for his next assignment at the company office. He arrived home pale as a ghost.

"What's wrong, dear?" said Mrs. Dodd, suddenly worried. "Did they fire you? Are you feeling all right?"

"The ship bound for India . . . remember?" he asked.

"Of course. How could I forget that dream I had?" she replied.

"The ship was torpedoed and sank," he declared. "All the men aboard escaped on a raft. They floated around in the ocean for sixteen days before they were finally picked up!"

Mrs. Dodd sat down. She was speechless.

"Your dream came true. You said I'd be hurt," he said quietly. "By stopping me from going, you may have saved my life!"

How could Mrs. Dodd have known that the ship would leave immediately for India and be sunk by a torpedo? Some people believe that her dream was a form of extra-sensory perception called precognition. She had a vision of the future. By taking action immediately, she prevented part of it from happening. The events of the dream took place, but without her husband.

Was it really ESP or just an unusual coincidence that happens now and then to people? No one knows for sure, but the Dodds will always be grateful.

The Bad Luck Diamond

A lot of bad luck has been linked over hundreds of years to the Hope diamond.

The diamond was mined from the Kistna River (now the Khrishna) in Golconda, India, in the fifteenth century. It was 112½ carats. (A carat is a unit of weight for gems equal to 200 milligrams.) Diamond rings worn on a person's finger are usually ½ to 1½ carats.

The diamond was placed in a Hindu temple and called the Hanuman, after the monkey god. According to one account, a Hindu priest stole the gem but was caught and killed for his crime.

In 1662, a French traveler, Jean Baptiste Tavernier, bought the diamond (though some say he stole it). Tavernier sold it to King Louis XIV of France. Louis had it cut down to 67 carats and called it the French Blue.

Meanwhile, Tavernier lost all his money and went into debt. He was eventually killed by a pack of wolves.

Nicolas Fouquet, a court official to Louis, borrowed the diamond to wear to a state ball. Then he was imprisoned for life after being convicted of embezzlement.

King Louis XVI gave the diamond to his Queen, Marie Antoinette. They both were beheaded by the guillotine in 1793 during the French Revolution.

Princess de Lamballe, a friend of Marie Antoinette's, often wore the diamond. She was later killed by a mob during the Revolution.

The stone then disappeared for almost forty years. Some say Catherine the Great of Russia wore it before her death. It was discovered again in London but had been cut down to 44½ carats.

One story says a Dutch diamond cutter reduced the stone and then killed himself. Another stated that a man named Fals sold it and then committed suicide.

The diamond ended up in the hands of Henry Philip Hope, a wealthy banker. It stayed in the Hope family for many years. Henry died of a stroke. His son went bankrupt and a grandson had to sell the jewel.

Other owners killed themselves, had unusual fatal accidents, or were murdered. The diamond was bought by the Sultan of Turkey in 1908 for $400,000. The businessman who sold the jewel to the Sultan drove off a cliff, killing his whole family.

The Sultan lost his throne and sold the diamond to the French jeweler Pierre Cartier. Cartier quickly sold it to businessman Ned McLean in 1911, and the Hope diamond moved to the United States.

McLean's wife, Evalyn Walsh McLean, wouldn't let her children touch the stone, which by now had a well-known reputation for bringing bad luck. The McLeans received letters asking them to get rid of it but they weren't worried. Perhaps they should have been!

During the nearly forty years that they owned the diamond, their eight-year-old son was killed by a car, Mrs. McLean became a drug addict, their daughter overdosed on sleeping pills, and Ed McLean went insane and died in an asylum.

The McLeans tried to sell the diamond. But they couldn't find a buyer who would pay enough (which wasn't surprising).

When Mrs. McLean died in 1947, jeweler Harry Winston bought her gem collection, which included the Hope diamond. While he owned it, Winston couldn't get life insurance from any company! They all believed so much in the evil reputation of the stone that they didn't think he had long to live.

Winston owned the diamond for eleven safe and uneventful years. Then he gave the stone away, the only owner to ever do such a thing. He donated it to the Smithsonian Institution in Washington, D.C., in 1958.

Today, the magnificent gem sits in the Hall of Jewels at the Smithsonian. The perfect blue stone is insured for one million dollars and lies in a case of bulletproof glass. Some say it hypnotizes those who gaze at it too long.

Why was so much death and misfortune linked to the Hope diamond?

Was it evil or cursed?

Was it just a string of coincidences?

Or was it human greed and selfishness that helped bring about the unfortunate events? No one knows for sure.

The Deepest Feeling

The Matthews family (not their real name) bought a beach house in Southern California. Mrs. Matthews, a nurse, took her three children to spend the weekend at the coast.

She planned to do some work on the house while the children played. The house was on a cliff overlooking the Pacific Ocean 150 feet below.

Mrs. Matthews was in the kitchen standing at the stove. She was browning a roast for dinner. Suddenly, she felt strongly that she should shut off the stove and go to the beach. The feeling was so deep and powerful that she shut off the gas immediately and walked out of the kitchen. Then, for some unexplained reason, Mrs. Matthews got her binoculars.

There were several levels of steep steps from the house. After walking about seventy-five feet down to the first level, Mrs. Matthews looked through the binoculars. In the distance, she saw one of the neighborhood children waving and jumping.

"Something is wrong," she thought to herself. "I'd better hurry." She ran down the remaining steps to the beach and over to the child.

The young girl pointed up to the cliff, where Mrs. Matthews saw two feet sticking out of the sand. Her breath caught in her throat. The children were playing on a ledge when it must have collapsed, burying them in sand and rocks.

"There's no time to get help," Mrs. Matthews thought. "They must get air soon or they'll die."

She climbed up the cliff and dug at the sand and rocks with her bare hands. Mrs. Matthews freed one child and then found a second and a third one completely buried.

Fighting exhaustion and somehow finding extra strength, she pushed boulders aside, dug the other children out, and dragged them onto the beach. They were unconscious, their faces blue and swollen from lack of oxygen.

Mrs. Matthews's training as a nurse took over. She cleaned out their throats, which were filled with candy and sand, and then applied mouth-to-mouth resuscitation.

Near collapse herself, she was able to revive all three children. Once they were breathing and out of immediate danger, Mrs. Matthews got help.

What strange feeling made her take her binoculars? Without them, she never would have seen the child waving for help in the distance.

Later, Mrs. Matthews explained that she was aware of "the deepest feeling" to go down to the beach. "I definitely feel I was sent there to do a job," she declared.

If she hadn't followed through on that feeling immediately, the children wouldn't have survived. "It wasn't a moment too soon," explained Mrs. Matthews.

Was it extrasensory perception? Or was it just a coincidence that made her head to the beach at that moment, binoculars in hand? Whatever it was, the heroic actions of Mrs. Matthews saved the lives of all three children.

A Single Red Rose

Sam was at his sister's house in the sitting room. He looked around and saw a metal coffin resting on two chairs. In the coffin was the dead body of a young boy.

"Oh, no! It's Henry," he thought to himself. "My brother is dead!"

Sam saw a bouquet of flowers on Henry's chest. It was unusual because the flowers were all white except for one red rose in the center.

Suddenly, Sam found himself wide awake and in bed. Upset about his brother's death, he dressed quickly and went for a walk. After Sam left the house, he realized that his brother Henry wasn't dead. He was still alive. It was just a dream that had seemed so real!

He went back to the house and was relieved to see the sitting room empty. He then told his sister about his frightening dream.

It was the late 1850s and Sam and Henry worked on

riverboats. They traveled the Mississippi River between St. Louis, Missouri, where they lived with their sister, and New Orleans, Louisiana.

The boys enjoyed the work and it was a thrill to visit different places along the river. There was always the possibility of danger on the big boats. Now and then, the boilers would explode and set off fires. Sometimes, the boat sank and crew and passengers 'were burned.

Sam and Henry worked on the riverboat *Pennsylvania*, which traveled to Memphis, Tennessee, and then to New Orleans. Henry stayed on board the *Pennsylvania* for the trip back to St. Louis. But Sam stayed over for two nights to explore and then took a different boat back.

On the trip home, at a stop in Greenville, Mississippi, Sam heard horrible news. The boilers on the *Pennsylvania* had exploded near Memphis. One hundred fifty people were killed! Henry was one of those who were badly injured.

Sam went to Memphis and visited Henry in the hospital. He had been severely burned by the boiling-hot steam from the exploding boilers. Unfortunately, Henry never recovered and died a few days later.

Sam went to see Henry's body one last time before it was buried. His brother was lying in a metal coffin. The other victims of the accident were buried in wooden coffins, but several Memphis women had donated money to buy a metal one for Henry. The coffin was resting on two chairs.

"It's just like in my dream," thought Sam sadly to himself, "but this time it's real and I'm not going to wake up in bed."

What about the bouquet of flowers? As Sam stood near the coffin, a woman entered the room and, without a word, gently placed a bouquet of white flowers on Henry's chest. There was one red rose in the middle!

Sam, whose full name was Samuel Clemens, grew up to be the famous writer, Mark Twain. He told others of his precognitive dream. It was a vision of the future which really came true.

Twain also believed in telepathy, another form of extra-sensory perception, and was a member of the Society for Psychical Research in London. Twain had several tele-pathic experiences of his own in which he believed that he was able to communicate with certain people by thoughts alone.

In one incident, Twain wrote a letter to a journalist named William Wright. Twain suggested that the journalist write a book on the rich silver mine that had just been discovered in Virginia City, Nevada, where Wright lived. But Twain put the letter aside and didn't mail it. He wanted to talk to his publisher first.

One week later, a letter to Twain arrived from Virginia City. Before opening the letter, Twain told a relative, "This is from William Wright and he wants to write a book on the big silver mine in Nevada."

Twain was correct! William Wright's letter was dated the *exact* day that Twain had written his letter and put it aside.

Was it mental telepathy that communicated Twain's idea about the book to William Wright? Or was it just a coin-cidence that Wright proposed the book idea on the exact day that Twain was thinking the very same thing?

Coincidence or Something More?

A coincidence is defined as the occurrence of events or things that seem related but have no actual connection in how they come about.

Everyone has had such experiences and wondered about them. Two people talk about a friend they haven't seen in ten years. Later in the day, that very same person sits next to them in a restaurant. "What a coincidence!" the friend says. Or is some other power involved?

Does extrasensory perception or the supernatural play a part in coincidence? You be the judge.

A number of amazing facts have linked two famous Presidents of the United States, Abraham Lincoln and John Fitzgerald Kennedy.

Lincoln was first elected to Congress in 1846. Kennedy was first elected to Congress in 1946, exactly one hundred years later.

Lincoln was elected President in 1860. Kennedy was elected President in 1960, exactly one hundred years later.

Both Presidents were assassinated on a Friday, with their wives sitting next to them.

Both men were killed by bullets in the back of the head.

Lincoln was shot in Ford's Theater. Kennedy was killed in a car made by Ford. It was a Lincoln convertible.

After their murders, both men were succeeded in office by southerners named Johnson.

President Andrew Johnson was born in 1808. President Lyndon Johnson was born in 1908, one hundred years later.

Both assassins, John Wilkes Booth and Lee Harvey Oswald, were southerners.

Booth was born in 1839 (though some sources say 1838) and Oswald was born in 1939, one hundred years later.

Both assassins were killed before they could be brought to trial.

Both Lincoln and Kennedy were very much involved in civil rights for black Americans.

The first name of Lincoln's personal secretary was John. The last name of Kennedy's personal secretary was Lincoln.

Both men had sons who died while they served as President.

Both names, Lincoln and Kennedy, have seven letters. The names of their Vice-Presidents, Andrew Johnson and Lyndon Johnson, have thirteen letters. The names of their assassins, John Wilkes Booth and Lee Harvey Oswald, have fifteen letters.

Are all these things the result of simple coincidence, or is it something more?

Warning of Danger

"Bob, don't go to the meeting tonight!" declared twenty-five-year-old Dave to his brother-in-law.

It was the summer of 1951, and the Johnson family (not their real name) had just finished dinner. Bob was due to attend a meeting in San Jose, California, about twenty-five miles from the family home.

"Don't be silly, Dave," said Bob. "I'm going to meet Jack and he'll drive me there."

"Please, Bob. I have a bad feeling about your going," explained Dave. "Just stay home this once. I can't shake the feeling. Something bad is going to happen if you go!" Dave started to cry suddenly.

"Get hold of yourself, Dave," said Bob. He had never seen his brother-in-law so upset.

Mrs. Johnson came over to comfort her grown son. "He'll be all right, Dave." She was more concerned about Dave acting so strange.

After about fifteen minutes, Dave began to feel better. "The feeling's gone now," he explained. "It's all right for Bob to go."

"That's great, Dave," said Bob angrily. "I've missed my ride with Jack because of you and now I have to drive my own car."

Dave was embarrassed at how he had behaved. "Twenty-five years old and crying!" he thought to himself. "And for no real reason—just a feeling I had."

Bob left for the meeting and, after a few minutes, was stuck in traffic.

"It's not my night," he thought. "First Dave makes me miss my ride, and now I'm in bumper-to-bumper traffic."

Bob tried to see what was causing the problem up ahead.

"It's probably an accident," he thought.

As he inched closer toward the main intersection in town, what he saw made him nearly faint. A car was totally wrecked and the driver was lying on the highway where he had been thrown from the car. The driver was dead, his head crushed in.

"Oh, no, it's Jack, it's Jack," whispered Bob. "I was supposed to be in that car with him." Bob held his head in his hands and started to sob quietly.

"I'd be dead, too," he thought. "Dave, he knew . . . he knew what was going to happen. Dave saved my life!"

Later, Bob found out that Jack's brakes had locked on one side. His car flipped up in the air and came down on the wrong side of the road. Then he was hit head-on by another car.

How did Dave know what would happen? Was it just a hunch, what many call intuition (knowing something without a particular reason)? Or was it extrasensory perception?

Whatever the explanation, Jack had Dave to thank for saving his life that night.

Execution by Bone

A young aborigine breaks one of the important laws of his tribe. Instead of appearing at the community court, he runs away. The court sentences him to death, and the executioner loads the killing-bone. The killers track him down.

One of them walks up close to the young man and drops to his knees. The bone is pointed at the man like a gun. The victim freezes in position. He's full of terror.

The killer says, "May your heart tear apart, your backbone be split, your ribs tear apart, your head and throat split open. You die, you die, you die!"

The killers leave. The young man believes that the bone is now inside his body, slowly destroying him. He tries to speak but can't make a sound. He foams at the mouth and falls to the ground. He screams and moans with pain. In a few days, he is dead.

Aborigines are the native people of Australia. For a long

time they were completely isolated from any outside human contact and lived in a very primitive way.

Their belief system includes forms of extrasensory perception and magic. Many use telepathy to communicate with other tribesmen and even with animals.

Execution by bone-pointing works because the aborigines *believe* it will work. This belief, which exists firmly in their minds, causes physical changes in the body. It slowly stops functioning, and death is the result.

An example of bone-pointing is given by John Godwin in his book *Unsolved—the World of the Unknown*. In 1953, an aborigine named Kinjika was sentenced to death, tracked down, and "pointed." He was flown three hundred miles to a modern hospital in Darwin, Australia. Doctors tried to save his life. But within five days, after much pain and suffering, Kinjika was dead.

Doctors found nothing wrong with him after X rays, blood tests, and other examinations. The bone of death is a psychic weapon. The only cure is if the victim believes that the doctor's medicine is more powerful than the magic of the tribal executioner, the *mulunguwa*.

The killing-bone (called the *kundela*) is usually a human bone, about eight inches long. Some tribes use the bone of an animal or one made of wood or stone. The bone is smooth with one pointed end. The other end has a hole in which the hair of a woman is braided.

The bone is loaded with magic power by the *mulunguwa* in a special ceremony. It is then pointed at the victim and no one else. Once the bone is pointed (and the victim believes it enters his body), the bone is burned.

If the victim runs away, he is hunted by the tribal killers, the *kurdaitcha*. They wear special slippers made of cockatoo feathers and human hair, which leave tracks only in soft sand. They cover themselves with human blood and then stick kangaroo hair and bird feathers to their body. This camouflages them so they're almost invisible.

Kurdaitcha will hunt a person for weeks, months, or even years until they corner him and point the bone.

The victim is doomed once the bone is pointed. Relatives and other tribal members treat the person as if he is already dead. It's only a matter of time before the end comes and the victim dies.

The doctor who signed Kinjika's certificate listed ''death by natural causes.''

Perhaps it should read, ''death by supernatural causes.''

Glossary

ABORIGINE: a native of Australia

ASSASSIN: murderer

CARAT: a unit of weight for gemstones equal to 200 milligrams

CLAIRVOYANCE: the ability to identify things without using the five basic senses (seeing, hearing, smelling, tasting, or touching)

COINCIDENCE: the occurrence of events or things that seem related but are not connected in how they come about

COMMERCIAL: the buying, selling, or trading of goods and services

EMBEZZLEMENT: the taking of another person's property or money as one's own

EXTRASENSORY PERCEPTION (ESP): knowledge gained from the "extra" senses other than the five basic senses

EXTRATERRESTRIAL: existing or coming from outside the earth

FIREBALL: a very bright meteor

GALLOWS: two upright posts and a crossbeam from which criminals are hanged

GUILLOTINE: a sharp-bladed machine used to cut off a person's head

INTERFERENCE: something which blocks or cuts off radio or television signals

INTUITION: the ability to know something without facts or reason to support it

MAMMALS: man and animals that feed mother's milk to their young and have skin covered with hair

MYTHOLOGY: supernatural stories and legends that try to explain certain beliefs, practices, or things in nature

NOOSE: a loop of thick rope with a running knot that tightens

PARAPSYCHOLOGY: the science of dealing with the "extra" senses that have no physical explanation, such as clairvoyance and telepathy

PRECOGNITION: the ability to see the future

RESUSCITATION: bringing back from unconsciousness or near death

SPECIMEN: a sample

TELEPATHY: the ability to communicate over any distance
from one mind to another without actually speaking
TORPEDO: underwater bomb

ZENER CARDS: a deck of twenty-five cards used in ESP
testing; each deck contains five circles, five squares,
five stars, five crosses, and five wavy lines

Bibliography

Allen, Martha Dickson. *Real Life Monsters*. Englewood Cliffs, New Jersey: Prentice-Hall, 1978.

Atkinson, Linda. *Psychic Stories—Strange But True*. New York: Franklin Watts, 1979.

Aylesworth, Thomas G. *ESP*. New York: Franklin Watts, 1975.

Aylesworth, Thomas G. *Science Looks at Mysterious Monsters*. New York: Julian Messner, 1982.

Baumann, Elwood D. *Monsters of North America*. New York: Franklin Watts, 1978.

Campbell, Elizabeth Montgomery, and Solomon, David. *The Search for Morag*. New York: Walker & Company, 1973.

Cohen, Daniel. *A Modern Look at Monsters*. New York: Dodd, Mead & Company, 1970.

Cohen, Daniel. *Monsters, Giants, and Little Men from Mars*. Garden City, New York: Doubleday & Company, 1975.

Cohen, Daniel. *The World of UFOs*. New York: J. B. Lippincott Company, 1978.

Costello, Peter. *In Search of Lake Monsters*. New York: Coward, McCann & Geoghegan, 1974.

David, Jay. *The Flying Saucer Reader*. New York: The New American Library, 1967.

Fitzgerald, Randall. *The Complete Book of Extraterrestrial Encounters*. New York: Collier Books, 1979.

Fowler, Raymond E. *Casebook of a UFO Investigator*. Englewood Cliffs, New Jersey: Prentice-Hall, 1981.

Fowler, Raymond E. *UFOS—Interplanetary Visitors*. Jericho, New York: Exposition Press, 1974.

Frazier, Kendrick. *Paranormal Borderlands of Science*. Buffalo, New York: Prometheus Books, 1981.

Frazier, Kendrick. *Science Confronts the Paranormal*. Buffalo, New York: Prometheus Books, 1986.

Godwin, John. *Unsolved—The World of the Unknown*. Garden City, New York: Doubleday & Company, 1976.

Hall, Elizabeth. *Possible Impossibilities*. Boston, Massachusetts: Houghton Mifflin Company, 1977.

Hartman, Jane. *Looking at Lizards*. New York: Holiday House, 1978.

Heaps, Willard A. *Psychic Phenomena*. New York: Thomas Nelson, 1974.

Hendry, Allan. *The UFO Handbook*. Garden City, New York: Doubleday & Company, 1979.

Hintze, Naomi A. and Pratt, J. Gaither. *The Psychic Realm—What Can You Believe?* New York: Random House, 1975.

Jacobs, David Michael. *The UFO Controversy in America*. Bloomington, Indiana: Indiana University Press, 1975.

Kettelkamp, Larry. *Investigating Psychics*. New York: William Morrow, 1977.

Keyhoe, Major Donald E. *Aliens From Space*. Garden City, New York: Doubleday & Company, 1973.

Klass, Philip J. *UFOs Explained*. New York: Random House, 1974.

Landsburg, Alan. *In Search of . . .* Garden City, New York: Nelson Doubleday, 1978.

Mackal, Roy P. *The Monsters of Loch Ness*. Chicago, Illinois: The Swallow Press, 1976.

Mayer, Ann Margaret. *Who's Out There?: UFO Encounters*. New York: Julian Messner, 1979.

Napier, John, *Bigfoot*. New York: E. P. Dutton, 1972.

Newton, Michael. *Monsters, Mysteries, and Man*. Reading, Massachusetts: Addison-Wesley, 1979.

Reader's Digest. *Mysteries of the Unexplained*. The Reader's Digest Association, 1982.

Reader's Digest. *Strange Stories, Amazing Facts*. The Reader's Digest Association, 1976.

Rhine, Louisa E. *Hidden Channels of the Mind*. New York: William Sloane Associates, 1961.

Rhine, Louisa E. *The Invisible Picture—A Study of Psychic Experiences*. Jefferson, North Carolina: McFarland & Company, 1981.

Rudley, Stephen. *The Abominable Snow Creature*. New York: Franklin Watts, 1978.

Shackley, Myra. *Still Living*? New York: Thames & Hudson, 1983.

Sheaffer, Robert. *The UFO Verdict*. Buffalo, New York: Prometheus Books, 1981.

Stevenson, Ian. *Telepathic Impressions—A Review and Report of 35 New Cases*. Charlottesville, Virginia: University Press of Virginia, 1970.

Story, Ronald D. *The Encyclopedia of UFOs*. Garden City, New York: Doubleday & Company, 1980.

The New York Times, May 26, 1979.

Vidal, Gore. *Lincoln*. New York: Random House, 1984.

White, Dale. *Is Something out There? The Story of Flying Saucers*. Garden City, New York: Doubleday & Company, 1968.

Wylie, Kenneth. *Bigfoot*. New York: The Viking Press, 1980.

HAGAR THE HORRIBLE